SOLILOQUIES

THAYIL EDITIONS

Forthcoming

My Dead Flowers | Buku Sarkar

happily ever after | Kamal Trilok Singh

Let the Smithereens | Karthika Naïr

'What does it mean to look in a mirror and find oneself transformed into a lizard? *Soliloquies* is not a sequel to Kafka's story but an experience that Adil Jussawalla had at seventeen, not long after which he wrote this play. Reading it today, after nearly seven decades, is as much an entry into an invisible literary history of transformative experience as it is a record of an early adulthood marked by spiritual unease, a condition now denied by a culture of containment and contentment. All literature is a relationship between parent and child, a questioning of the father—this verse drama begins with a father, a "bastard father"; and as I read on, through the alliterative rhythm of "dissolution, darkness, despair", and as pairs kept appearing and disappearing, changing in form but not pattern, traversing shadow and light, the known and unknown, obedience and command, truth and lies, response and responsibility, God and Un-God, I occasionally heard the impress of Eliot's pairs that fall between shadows in *The Hollow Men* and *Murder in the Cathedral*, and I paused to recognize the pain of never knowing anything in its entirety, what Jussawalla condenses into a line as prayer: "Heal this pain of division, Lord". This is soliloquy like sleep is soliloquy, made beautiful by the honesty of relinquishing control. It is deeply moving to read a seventeen-year-old boy admit, with great knowledge, that everything, but more particularly the past, its voices, "remains unknown for me and earth". I reread *Soliloquies* immediately after reading it the first time, perhaps from the need to comfort a young Adil that he indeed was "still too young to go to Hell". I think the truth is that I reread it to discover the language of the fidgetiness of my own soul—"the hurt of a part".'

Sumana Roy

SOLILOQUIES

ADIL JUSSAWALLA

FOURTH ESTATE · *New Delhi*

First published in India by Fourth Estate 2025
An imprint of HarperCollins *Publishers*
By arrangement with Thayil Ink
HarperCollins *Publishers* India, Cyber City, Building 10-A, Gurugram,
Haryana – 122002, India
www.harpercollins.co.in

2 4 6 8 10 9 7 5 3 1

Hand-drawn charcoal text by Dharini Bhaskar

P-ISBN: 978-93-6989-362-1
E-ISBN: 978-93-6989-003-3

Typeset in 11/15.5 Aldine401 BT at
HarperCollins *Publishers* India

Printed and bound at
Replika Press Pvt. Ltd.

MIX
Paper | Supporting responsible forestry
FSC™ C016779

This book is produced from independently certified FSC® paper to ensure responsible forest management.

HarperCollins *Publishers*, Macken House, 39/40 Mayor Street Upper,
Dublin 1, D01 C9W8, Ireland

Me

London

Drawing by Hiroko, student*, 1968.
* Hiroko was a classmate of Veronik's at the International Language Centre on Shaftesbury Avenue, London, where I used to teach.

A Conversation with Adil Jussawalla

THAYIL EDITIONS (TE): How old were you when you wrote *Jian*?

ADIL JUSSAWALLA (AJ): I was either seventeen or eighteen. *Jian* was my first full-length play. I was living in London at that time. I think one of the factors that led to it was that I was suffering from a breakdown without really knowing it, or I knew about it, and could have named it as such. Let's just say it was the deprivation of food and the lack of a sexual life, and feeling overworked at my college of architecture. My breakdown was such that I looked into the mirror and thought I'd turned into a lizard. When I left my bedsitter in Dollis Hill in northwest London, and went to the park near it, Gladstone Park, there were all these thoughts. I recalled my own dependence on religious thought in my boyhood. I was brooding about an uncle of mine who had given up his naturopathic practice and become a guru of sorts in Bombay. These thoughts suddenly led to the most incredible experience. I was lying on my back in the park, and I felt myself merging into the sky and the grass. I was undergoing something so ecstatic that when the tears flowed, it was because I wanted it to stop. It was too much to take. I would call this a primary mystical experience, and I've never had a similar one. There are those who are agnostic or atheist, even believers, who had similar experiences of extreme ecstasy. It happens suddenly, not necessarily lying down in a park. The experience is not unusual. But this thing about never seeing the face of God again, which is the anguish that John Donne expresses in one of his works, that was the worst experience—that you will not have that feeling again and will be very far from God. We can use the name God, because when one reads mystical literature, God both exists and does not exist. This anguish and torment, the withdrawal from that experience, I don't know if it's like the withdrawals and depression that follow substance-induced highs. There was a teacher who studied Buddhist and early Indian thought in London called P.D. Mehta. He was my first piano teacher in Bombay, but he left for London and taught at a school there. His thinking about religion was drawing followers at the time. He was known to be reliable on Buddhism and holistic thought. When I was in trouble, in a spiritual crisis, I visited him. He said he didn't believe in heaven or hell as actual places and that no one knows what happens after death because no one has returned. But he said this being forever excluded from the sight of God, forever to be seeing things as through a glass darkly, and never to see his face again, he said that *that* is hell. I think there's a great deal of truth in that, because even those who are disillusioned by mullahs and theologians still seek for a truth that is valid, a feeling that this is real—the mystical experience. You hope to get it again because it seems to be more real than the humdrum life you are leading. There seems to be the need of what I can only call the soul to find satisfaction or to find meaning. However wise you may become in the process, there is this longing for more. I don't think you can dismiss mysticism as obfuscation. Of course, there are corrupt godmen and priests and mystics, but there is an alternate truth there which is not really provided for by just following ritual, however closely you follow it. I think some of this you may find when you look at the soliloquies in the text, the intense darkness that comes over Jian when he speaks.

TE: Jian's soliloquies are in free verse, and they read very much like poems.

AJ: It's not as though when I was going through this difficult time, impoverished in every way in London, I hadn't written free verse. I discovered I was so caught up in the internal turbulence of my protagonist Jian, that when he's not talking to members of his family, he gives vent to his thoughts in soliloquies. I found that the soliloquies were naturally forming themselves in free verse, whereas the rest of the play was in dialogue.

TE: Is Jian representative of the mystic figure, or one who would be a mystic?

AJ: Jian is a seedbed for mysticism, a would-be mystic who renounces his family. He leaves the house and surrenders to another kind of reality. I think why I had someone like him as a protagonist is because he reflected some of my own background. I was influenced by the Bible. And, being brought up in India, you couldn't avoid hearing about various gurus who were supposed to guide you to salvation. So, these religious influences are the background to this character Jian.

For many years, I've been anxious not to get overloaded with copies and originals of my own work. The flat would just be overrun. Once I found a couple of places where

I could offload the originals of my texts, I did that. I sent a copy of *Jian*, the play, to SCILET and much later to Cornell, but before that I got a few copies of the soliloquies made because I wanted to refer to them from time to time, also thinking that they might come in useful later. I'm glad that's happening now. The disadvantage is that I cannot fully recollect the plot of the play. To reduce the importance of that, I could generalize by saying the play is about a young man's discontent with so-called family values and religion as have been practised in the household. He wants to find the truth for himself. Having had what he regards as a mystical experience, he'd like to test out the truth of it in the bigger world. It happens in other structures, not just family—in academia, in religious institutions, the church, rituals, theological information—the emphasis on the father, son and holy ghost. What does that trinity mean? What is the virgin birth? The answers from these institutions are not enough, so she or he will have to find out for themselves, which often entails breaking away from these institutions, or leaving them.

TE: Did your reading at the time have any bearing on the play?

AJ: Colin Wilson's *The Outsider*, since I already felt an outsider in England; being isolated, feeling I was a foreigner there. Wilson was an outsider in a different sense, and I felt drawn to that particular book and its philosophy.

TE: How long did it take you to write?

AJ: Couldn't have been longer than three or four months. The play failed to get a producer interested. It was obviously unstageable, with these long soliloquies. I told you about my breakdown. I was writing poems then in free verse. There was one that was not in free verse, part of which I recall from memory, though some words I'm unable to recall. It's called 'Hampstead Heath' and, oh gosh, yes, I must have written the poem in the winter of 1959 or early 1960. What I have is this:

> Last summer's trees, changed to giant feathers,
> Splayed in cold formations, pierce the ground;

Remembrance spears my face. The bare mound
On which I sit and trace my shifting weathers
To a sun now gone is far from where
Muddy children wage a playtime war
And all their glorious dying mocks, reproves
My own. Sandcastles fall as sand. Now nothing moves.

Around the pond stand houses of three winters'
Seeing, each winter spent in England changed.
[words missing] from faith and hope estranged,
My tongue ran dry, my senses broke in splinters.
Now I must learn to trust again, to make
From fractured things a landscape of my own.
[words missing] new shapes reform and break
[words missing] and a new horizon.

Does every conifer plant survive
The blades of ice? What saplings lying chopped?
The pulse of light around the water's stopped.
Oh earth, awake! As boys in denims drive

The swans away and fish knee-deep in scum,
The pond's blind upwards staring I reject,
And make believe another kingdom's come,
Another land ...

It never got finished. I think I got some lines right. I never published it because I never brought it to a conclusion.

TE: Did your mystical experience lead to a knowledge of, a union with God?

AJ: I told you of the experience of being lifted off the grass into another dimension when I was lying on my back in Gladstone Park, which is close to where I was living at that time, in a rented room. What I distinctly remember is feeling the stars coming closer and closer to me and brighter and brighter in a way that was ... what they were telling me silently was ... *look kid, you're all right, we are always here*. Because if you remember, I told you I was not eating well, I wasn't feeling well, I'd had a breakdown. The central point of that experience is that the lifting up of my spirit was not an out-of-body experience. I just felt the stars were coming closer to me and saying this and that when I wanted the experience to stop, when the tears were flowing. There was confirmation in that, the stars were confirming my existence; the people around me were not. The stars were giving me confidence to carry on. It wasn't what the mystics call a union with God or anything like that. If I had let that experience continue, it would have gone to a higher level. What I do remember writing to my father, when he was upset I'd left architecture, I remember saying, I have seen God. And my mother reported to me later that my father said: But is it that easy to see God? He was very skeptical. Over time, I wouldn't say I had that great mystical experience of union with God.

TE: Are you still interested in mysticism?

AJ: I'm reading Simon Critchley's *On Mysticism.* He concentrates on the Christian mystics, Julian of Norwich and others. He doesn't go anywhere near Eastern mysticism.

TE: Probably a wise thing.

AJ: There was a book, *Mysticism Sacred and Profane* by R.C. Zaehner. Critchley doesn't cite him. I wonder if it's because Zaehner suggests there are kinds of mysticism that are linked to mental illness. I think Critchley dismisses biological sickness in some mystics and their experiences.

From the Bible, what I have from memory is: *In the beginning was the Word, and the Word was with God*. What Critchley does, in explaining either Julian of Norwich or Meister Eckhart, he says something very interesting, that the Word was silent. The Word doesn't speak until you tell it to speak, until you enter the Word. The Word doesn't come to us, you can't share it, it's silent, but once you enter it through a mystical experience, it speaks to you. Our experience when we pray, through desperation, as Emily Dickinson discovered, is that God doesn't reply. But when you have that mystical experience, when you penetrate the Word, it begins to speak of things mystical. You negate, you negate, you negate—the use of Buddhist words: not this, not that, not that—until you experience the mystical. Think of Keats's idea of negative capability. I was astonished to find a poem by Donne which says the same thing. How can things which do not exist help in rebirth? These are Donne's words: 'and I am re-begot / Of absence, darkness, death: things which are not.'

TE: You told me once that as a boy you had the nickname 'Buster Keaton'.

AJ: If you want nicknames, shall we start with the first? I was a forceps kid. I didn't want to get into the world. I was pulled out by none other than Dr Shirodkar, who was also responsible for the birth of Saleem Sinai, aka Salman Rushdie. My first nickname, when my father's mother saw me with that distorted face, was Quasimodo, which didn't go down well with my mother. Eventually, the top of my head flattened out, but I can't help the long face. I was called Buster Keaton by Mr Pharaoh, the mathematics teacher. If he tried to make a joke, the whole class would laugh loudly. You had to be in his good books. I'd keep a straight face, which is exactly what Keaton did—chaos all around him and his straight face. He had another nickname for me, Atlas, because I was the quiet one. He'd say, 'There you are carrying the world's worries on your shoulders.' Then, there was another nickname, not so affectionate. My father, in the early fifties, had become quite well known for his nature cure clinic which stressed physical fitness—so he was chosen to be among the judges for one of the first Miss India contests. It was held at Brabourne Stadium and the award was given to Indrani Rahman. Clearly there was a school grapevine, because one day Mr Pharaoh began to call me Beauty Contest. I remember his looking around the class, which was sniggering. He didn't approve of women parading in swimming costumes and didn't realize my father was more puritanical than he. At home, we mostly spoke Gujarati, occasionally English, the latter becoming more pronounced from my father's side, having put me and my brother in an English-medium school. One of my mother's nicknames for me, borrowed from *Snow White*, was Grumpy, when I didn't respond to conversation. I was never much of a talker, I liked to be on my own. And I must have been slow in my movements as a child, because she used to call me *gokalgai*, the Gujarati word for 'snail'.

TE: As a schoolboy, you had to change your writing orientation from left to right.

AJ: I think I was sent to school when I was two and a half years old. A nun at that school, rather massive in her grey habit, must have noticed that I was using my left hand to write. She must have used some stern methods or words to make me start writing with my right hand, perhaps she thought that would exorcise the devil that had possessed me. The reorientation has affected my sense of direction. I find myself taking wrong turns. I get lost in new cities. Even when I recollect things, I remember them in another way rather than in the direction in which they happened. My mother noticed that something was wrong because I would start crying when it was time to go to school. She and my father decided then that I shouldn't go to Villa Theresa and put me into a school called Hill Grange. I have a memory of the arrangement the school made for students to take a nap between classes. Students got marks for sleeping soundly. I used to score the highest.

TE: You were interested in drawing from an early age.
AJ: I don't think school had much to do with my interest in drawing and colours. I have very distinct recollections of the sketches or drawings I tried to make of birds and boats. I don't know for what reason, but I was a silent child, so there was a comfort and joy in drawing and in trying to put down colours with crayons. My sense of being separate from the world of words may have had something to do with the fact that in the early forties my parents separated twice. Me and my mother were living at her sister's place on Altamount Road and my father would drop in for a visit from time to time. I drew the birds on my aunt Freny's balcony. I felt somehow isolated and this was a way of grounding myself. This continued because my mother herself had been in Santiniketan in the early thirties and had been taught by Nandalal Bose. She had to give up after a year because there were no funds to support

her. But she used to paint, so she naturally felt happy that I was doing this on my own. When things were normal between her and my father, she'd encourage me to send hand-painted cards to relatives and friends on birthdays. In school, not being (to put it mildly) a competitive sportsman, I was often left out of teams for this or that game and I'd content myself with drawing. I made stick figures in a sequence, telling a story, and I discovered that my getting back at adults (which continues even in my eighty-third year) is by making caricatures of them in drawings. Later, my writings in the compositions we were assigned at Cathedral School began to be noticed by some teachers. I used to get good marks, but I never felt I would write as a career or vocation. It was just that I liked shaping things with paints and pencils and crayons, and I liked shaping things with words. I guess that continues. I think things reached a head during what should have been my last year in school with the Senior Cambridge exam. The only reason I topped the class that year is that I got very high marks from the examiners on my artwork and essays. In my last year at Cathedral, we had a colourful teacher by the name of Lady Temple. Quite a legend. I think she really was a Lady but I'm not sure how she got that honour; she never talked about her husband. She'd be what we dismiss as eccentric. She encouraged the class to paint on large sheets of paper, not the small sketch pads we were normally given, large sheets of thickish paper meant for gouache, coloured paper, grey or blue sheets that we got from Bombay Stationery Mart.

TE: How and when did you first begin to write?

AJ: It was around the same time I'd been given a diary from one of my father's patients to write down my thoughts, so I got increasingly interested in doing that. I was fourteen, then, and began to make notes about the films I'd seen, certain daily events. This kind of diary-keeping continued from 1954 to 1958, so I guess it meant something to me. The other thing was, two teachers of very different temperaments appreciated my class work, Alan Glynne-Howell and C.J. Oliver, so I got increasingly interested not in what I was saying but in how I was saying it; in style and form. I also wrote a short story for the school magazine and some satirical verse. I'd been made a prefect and what could I do but make fun of prefects? I didn't think of poetry at all seriously.

Then, in my school-leaving year, 1955, they decided to introduce a two-year course, the Higher School Certificate (HSC). Whoever opted to take it would have got what the British call A levels. At that time, A levels seemed to have become indispensable if you wanted to get into a university in the UK. I was put under a lot of pressure by the principal, and maybe my father, to take the course. Instead of going straight to college in Bombay which I could have done, or if I had more faith in my painting abilities, perhaps an art school, I glumly agreed to be part of this small HSC class. Was it masochistic? I don't know. The good thing was we had quite a remarkable teacher imported specially for the class, Rider Salmon. He opened up the world of modern literature for the six students in his class; one of them was Anjolie Dev, who also excelled in painting and became Anjolie Ela Menon. Mr Salmon opened for us the poems in the *Penguin Book of Contemporary Verse*. It was new, then. I'd never read stuff like that. Mr Salmon also introduced us to Eliot's *Murder in the Cathedral* and Virginia Woolf's *Orlando*. For other reasons, I was unhappy being in Bombay. I guess I missed the illusory freedom we're supposed to get after leaving school and going to college, and here I was, stuck for two years in a school I often hated. The ethos of Cathedral School wasn't suited to a dreamer like me. Nor perhaps to Anjolie. There was talk, 'You have an artistic bent of mind.' But unspoken was the idea that it wouldn't get us anywhere.

TE: How did you end up in an architecture course in London?

AJ: We heard of the Architectural Association School of Architecture (AA), very well known, and the good thing from my point of view was that it didn't require A levels. I thought I wouldn't continue with HSC, I'd aim to get into the AA. Of course, there was much heartburn at school. Mr Salmon said, 'I've only met one other student who

AA School of Architecture, London, 1957
Photograph by Adil Jussawalla

wrote as well as you and he's now in Cambridge, stay on.' But I decided not to. Ironically, after landing in London, the AA School was a mixed experience. They threw us into the deep end. They didn't teach theories of structure, we were to experiment—building models, drawing plans, etc. It was fun, but the hours were long and I was living in digs far away with no time to write. I couldn't keep up my diary. After the exhilarating taste of modern writing at Cathedral, I needed to read more poetry.

The theatre scene, angry young men, Campaign for Nuclear Disarmament protests: there was a lot of excitement in the late fifties. After my eighteenth birthday, I felt architecture was not for me, my heart was in writing free verse. My isolation left me with little option but to find release in writing. Because of the new theatre scene in London, particularly at the Royal Court Theatre in Sloane Square, where Osborne had the first performance of *Look Back in Anger* a couple of years before, I felt I'd write *Jian*, about renouncing family, set in an invented land, northern, Scandinavian, the setting influenced by Ibsen. A young man, with a priest for his father, meditates a lot and finally decides to leave home. Those meditations, which were soliloquies, emerged naturally as free verse. The dialogues were in conversational prose. Again, it showed that the writing of poems had me in its grip. I sent it here and there, the Royal Court, etc. The professional typist who typed it up was aghast at how young I was. She asked, 'You wrote the play?' It was nice getting praise like that. What else she thought of it I don't know, but I know she was impressed. Of course, it got nowhere. There were other kinds of poems, totally unrelated, that I began to write. You may have noticed that in quite a lot of poems, I use the dramatic monologue, a tree may speak, unlikely things may speak, and that feeling, for that kind of poem, continues.

Having rejected A levels in Bombay, I found I had to get them in England. I didn't have the spirit or the courage to abandon all thought of getting money from my parents. The government allowed six hundred pounds a year and with that I paid for architecture school, meals, and my rent. If I decided, look, I want to learn about theatre-craft and work backstage, I'll rough it out ... that money would have stopped. I didn't have the nerve. It was like a chakravyuha, I didn't know how to get out of it. I thought I couldn't keep dropping out, though of course I dropped out after my first year at Oxford, too. I'm the original hippie. Long before it became fashionable, I kept dropping out of things. I don't regret it, but obviously it caused a lot of pain to my parents. I was eighteen and I'd given up architecture. I was depressed after the failure of my play. Since I knew I couldn't make it on my own without funds from India, I had to get into an educational institution. I went on someone's recommendation to Felsham House in Suffolk. It would give me the coaching I needed for A levels and whatever the higher educational institutions wanted. It was a boarding place. After a year there, I had to sit for the common entrance exam for Oxford and Cambridge. University College, Oxford, accepted me. By then I was writing poems.

TE: Let's talk about how your first book of poems, *Land's End*, came about.

AJ: The good thing about Felsham, a village, was that, though I missed the anonymity and the cosmopolitan life of London, there was nature, walks in its fields and woods, which the poems in *Land's End* reflect. The last poem is about the view from my room on Merton Street, Oxford. When I did get into Oxford, I was older than most of the students, so I was put into a house with postgraduate students. I was cut off from college life. I'd left Bombay in 1957 and at the end of my second term in 1960, Oxford had Prelims, exams we had to pass to get into our second year. One of the tutors for Old English was Christopher Tolkien who used to look at us as if we were rabble that had invaded his domain. He wasn't used to teaching. I mention this only to recount a series of failures. Predictably, I failed in Old English and Latin, which meant I would have to try again. I was sick of failing. I decided that Oxford, England, too, is not for me, I'll go back to Bombay. By then, I'd spent four years in England without getting a degree or qualifications for a career. My father, when I returned to Bombay without a degree, said this felt like a death sentence. I'd thrown away a great opportunity. My grandmother, his mother, had proudly told him no one in the family had been to Oxford. There was great disappointment. I was staying at my parents' place and I wanted to get into a college here, but they wouldn't take me unless I did my Inter Arts, which would have meant another year gone, and two more before I got a degree. So then, meekly, I wrote to Oxford. Will you have me back? And they said, yeah, come back. While I was in Bombay, I'd meet Nissim Ezekiel. He lived in a paying guest apartment nearby, at Warden Road. I showed him the manuscript of poems I'd written. He said he'd just been published by P. Lal and would send the manuscript to him. Lal accepted it and that's how *Land's End*, published by Lal's Writers Workshop, came about. In London, there was a student, Chris Oastler, who was hardly a friend, who had been with me at the school of architecture, who also landed up at Felsham, and also at Univ, which was amazing. He had an eye for art and took one look at the cover and said, 'What's that cabbage leaf doing, the Writers Workshop logo?' He said he'd make a cover and include the quotes I'd got from reviews in India. So that's how the black-and-white cover for *Land's End* happened. One thing I told Chris was that I wanted the word 'Poems' in red but he said that couldn't be done, too expensive. I used to take a red marker and colour in that word in the copies I gave to people, in Oxford and its bookshops.

TE: You wrote other plays as well.

AJ: While I was at Felsham, I wrote a second play called *Floodwaters*, a verse drama. There were attempts to revive verse drama in the late fifties. This time, I set the play in India. The theme is an issue that has grown more and more relevant, the displacement of villagers in honour of big dams. The engineer in charge is a somewhat arrogant guy and there's a rebellion. Can you imagine all of them talking in verse in English? Chris said, 'You have these villagers talking in South Kensingtonese!'

It wasn't quite as bad as all that. But since I'm recounting failures, I'll include this as one of them.

When I decided to leave architecture, my father asked E.M. Forster to intervene and drill some sense into my head. He was kind enough to give me an appointment. There was a party going on, a number of tall men, and Forster came over from that group and sat me down on a sofa. I'd sent him *Jian*, an invented name that I wanted to sound Scandinavian. I apologized and said, 'I don't see why you should take the trouble.' He was very kind, he heard me out. But after he read the play, he wrote to advise me to go back to architecture. In Felsham, I had an appointment with Angus Wilson. He lived there and I'd sent him *Jian*. He wasn't dismissive, but he said the subject—religion, renunciation and spirituality—wasn't something he was interested in. He said he appreciated what I was saying. I asked him to be more critical. He said, 'The point is I got what you were saying and that's what is important.' That comment stayed with me. Perhaps that's what one should be saying to people with first-time manuscripts that aren't quite there.

I got through the finals at Oxford and there was nothing to do but find work in London. The usual things: odd jobs, trying to sell encyclopaedias, cleaning carpets, etc. I got my degree in 1964 and that year itself, I was in London looking for jobs. For a while, I was put up in the attic room of a posh house in South Kensington. The person living in the rest of the house was Jill Hugh-Jones, wife of Stephen Hugh-Jones, who was perhaps the first literary editor of *The Indian Express*. Ramnath Goenka, the owner, didn't know what to make of him. On one of the book review pages, Stephen published a photograph of Allen Ginsberg, nude, having a bucket bath on a roof. After Jill and Stephen got back to London, their marriage was on the rocks. Jill had been given temporary residence in this mansion-like place. She let me stay in the attic room for free. Very kind of her—I can't forget that—and then I saw an ad in *The New Statesman* for an English language teaching course at a place called International House on Shaftesbury Avenue. With a diploma I'd be able to teach English, I thought. I didn't have the money to pay for the course and borrowed the ten guineas I needed from Farrukh Dhondy.

TE: Do you still owe him ten guineas?

AJ: No. But in his memoir *Fragments Against My Ruin* (2021), he says he borrowed money from me. Tricks of memory, I suppose. After getting my diploma, I got a job at the International Language Centre at International House and it paid me well enough to give up the odd jobs and move out of the attic room in Pelham Crescent. While I was teaching, I was also writing. I began a novel, which I had to abandon—another failure. Part of that novel has been published in the collection *I Dreamt a Horse Fell from the Sky* (2016). I did write a number of short stories and a radio play, but I destroyed them. They didn't go anywhere. I think it was in 1964 that Farrukh went to Cambridge and got involved as co-editor of a journal, *Carcanet*. It began as a joint venture of Oxford and Cambridge. Someone decided on a special Indian issue and Farrukh published at least two of my poems, 'The Raising of Lazarus' and 'Karate'. The Lazarus poem was dedicated to the poet Adrian Husain and takes an unusual look at Christ. I portray Christ as being quite disdainful of Lazarus. There is an element to the poem that might be described not so much as homoerotic but as homosadistic. In the course of my work at International House, I found myself teaching a number of rebels who gave the other teachers a great deal of trouble. One of them was Veronik Joannides. She'd been living in different places in London because she had decided to separate from her husband Jean in Paris. She came to London with her daughter Katia to learn English, a change of track. She'd trained to be a ballet dancer and an actress. She wasn't the ringleader of the troublemakers but somehow, in their attitudes they made it known that they didn't want to cooperate very much with the other teachers. I had a conversation class, which meant I had to get them to speak in English.

TE: Was this when you had long hair and looked a bit of a hippie?

AJ: I must have. The class consisted mostly of Europeans, some of whom were trying to be waiters in London. One or two were highly educated. It was quite a mix. What

View from Veronik's bed-sit on Campden Hill Road, London W.8, April 1968

COPY

initially shocked the European students was my informal wear. This was the sixties in England when things were freeing up. I was still more the angry young man of the fifties, but I did allow myself flared trousers and a colourful shirt, unheard of in Europe for a teacher to wear. A green or orange shirt. What next, I think, must have alarmed them was my Nehru jacket with paisley prints. On first seeing me, Veronik let out a discreet whoop in the ear of her good friend Anna, because she thought I was a Red Indian. Veronik and I danced together at the school's Christmas party—this must have been 1966—and then we met more often for a while. I even moved into her digs in Campden Hill Road, just off High Street, Kensington. I made a sketch of the view from her bedsit. Katia was in a school nearby and not

Katia, Ballerina
Photograph by
Adil Jussawalla

liking it, poor thing, having to learn English from scratch. She was five or six years old. Veronik enrolled her in the Rambert School of Ballet, and also in an ice-skating school. While skating, Katia slipped and broke her right arm. The arm was in plaster for a while. That is when the caretaker of the apartments in that building, Madame Kavalis, who was Greek (ironically, given that Katia was half-Greek), reported us to a department that responds to neglect of children, etc. I imagine that Madame Kavalis wasn't at all happy about my presence in the apartment of a married woman and her child. I don't think there was anything racial about it. One of these social service workers turned up at our door expecting a neglected child and cold parents but was pleasantly surprised. We got a clean chit. It could have gone either way if the social worker was racist. Then we moved house together, in 1967, to a bedsit in Pembroke Place, off High Street, Kensington. Fairly posh, though not High Street posh. We were on a floor above a bakery: two small rooms and a kitchen, with a tub for bathing in the kitchen itself.

Adil and Katia in London, 1968/69
Photograph by Veronik Jussawalla

TE: You befriended the poet Lawrence Bantleman around this time.

AJ: He is part of this story. He was passing through London on his way to Canada and we couldn't put him up. Farrukh and Mala said he could stay with them. There was some tension there. Later, in 1970, when Veronik, Katia and I were in India, Larry stayed at Pembroke Place. When Veronik got back, she found an enormous telephone bill, so he wasn't popular with her either. My one and only LSD trip was the one Larry introduced me to. It must have been in 1969, at Farrukh and Mala's, when he was staying there. Farrukh took one, Larry did and I did. Not Mala and not her sister, Kum. The whole thing was totally unsupervised. I was a complete newcomer. Maybe Farrukh had dropped acid before and Larry certainly had. I went off on my own into the streets of London and found I couldn't make my way home. It was like one's first experience of hell, as if one would be there forever. Farrukh must have been with me for a while, he said I went into pubs and said hello to everyone. But after he left, I couldn't find my way back.

Something kicked in. Guided not by heavenly lights but by street lights, I did find my way back and found everyone concerned. Larry was in a stupor in an armchair, dead to the world. I must have been babbling. I remember the alarmed look on Kum's face. I've never dared try LSD again.

TE: You edited the influential anthology *New Writing in India*. How did that come about?
AJ: I decided to revisit India in 1967. My first time was in 1961, when I left Oxford. Now, six years later, I went back. I wanted to see my parents. It was election year and I felt the pull of Bombay. Then I went back to my job in London. Maybe it was in 1968 that I got the idea it was high time the British knew something about our recent writing and writers. Penguin had started its series with *Italian Writing Today* and I was pretty impressed by that anthology. They followed it with one or two others. I had some recent writing with me, chapters of Nirad Chaudhuri, he wasn't well known at that time, and Ramanujan's poems, and I sent them to Penguin saying it was a sample, would they

be interested? The person in charge was Giles Gordon and he politely said no, they were not interested and that was that. I had a contemporary at Oxford who was working at André Deutsch, and he said he knew a person at Penguin who was now in charge of this series, Jill Norman. He said he'd put in a word. I did go to meet her. She said this series is doing very badly. We've been let down by the person we commissioned to do *Russian Writing Today*, but go ahead. By then, I must have also included 'Naipaul's India and Mine' by Nissim, because he had published that review in *Imprint* after *An Area of Darkness* (1964) came out.

I wasn't unknown in London. I read at the Poetry Society and was part of the Commonwealth Arts Festival readings in 1965. Dom Moraes didn't take to Adrian Husain's reading. We were standing outside the theatre. I think he was going to a party. He saw Adrian and said, 'I don't understand, his poems just seem to be about knives and forks.' He had a column in *The Times of India* at the time and that's exactly what he wrote in the column. In London, from time to time, Dom and I would run into each other. So maybe Jill Norman had heard of me through the grapevine. I realized I couldn't make this anthology sitting in London and that's when I decided to come to India, in 1970. The contract was signed in 1968. It was meant to be a temporary visit. Katia and Veronik came with me, it was their first time in India. We went on a kind of Bharat Yatra, meeting writers, and it was a different, exhilarating time. There wasn't this extreme antagonism between English-wallahs and language-wallahs; the bhasha writers were very cooperative. A slight caveat, I don't deny they were cooperative because there was a possibility of their work appearing abroad with Penguin. If that hadn't been there, would they have behaved differently? The anthology took a long time to come out. It was published in 1974. I never saw an advance copy. The first time I saw it was at one of the pavement bookstores on Hornby Road in Bombay. I did get a shock when I saw the cover. I'd sent them a selection of paintings. I expected a contemporary painter like Gulammohammed Sheikh and they had used a Bollywood poster with Jaya Bachchan on it. The painters

Veronik Jussawalla
Photograph by Adil Jussawalla

I'd recommended to Penguin were outraged. I found it all very funny. In the London days, between 1964 and 1969, I'd met Gulam and Vivan Sundaram. I also used to meet Geeta Kapur and F.N. Souza, and the person I met the most was Souza's half-brother Lancelot Ribeiro. When Veronik and I were at Pembroke Place, Vivan lent us a gigantic canvas of his to hang on our walls. Gulam also gave us a painting. After I got back to India, we did keep in touch. Gulam started a little magazine, *Vrishchik*, which means 'scorpion' in Gujarati, that he asked me to write for.

TE: Bombay in the seventies: a heady time. Tell me about the books Clearing House published. Was there a sense of community among the Bombay poets of the time?

AJ: I don't know if there was a feeling of community, at least that's not what I got. Nissim's office at PEN was a meeting ground for informal readings. I suppose what we shared was a sense of being beleaguered. We had no idea who was reading us. By the seventies, the people I knew were in their thirties and we were being influenced by different things. It was a time of upheaval in terms of ideologies—feminism in America, gay liberation. I can't think of a central place where poets in Bombay met and shared ideas. It happened in little islands, around Dom, for example, and Nissim.

As to how Clearing House was formed: we did find that quite a few of us had manuscripts ready and no publisher to send them to. I knew that Keki Daruwalla had a manuscript, I had one, Arvind had one, Kersy Katrak had another. But it began with just four of us, mainly due to logistics. Gieve Patel, Arvind Krishna Mehrotra, Arun Kolatkar and myself. One day, the four of us had been in the living room of my flat, in 1975, and we said let's just go ahead with the four of us. Too much time had gone by. We thought the best way of funding a publishing house would be to send out fliers for pre-order at a hefty discount to people we knew, to universities and so on. It was very clear that Arun would be in charge of design and production, Gieve would help with the proofs, I'd be the general dogsbody, and Arvind, with his sharp eye and comments, even when he was in Allahabad, would keep us going, the driving force. That's how Clearing

House brought out its first four books in 1976, *Jejuri*, *Nine Enclosures*, *How Do You Withstand, Body* and *Missing Person*. If Gieve had an idea, he'd stubbornly stick to it. He wanted a purely typographic cover. But when he saw what Arun had done for Arvind's book, he said, I want Arun to design it. Because I had to deal with the printers, I mumbled and grumbled and cursed but that was the way it went. Inland Printers were happy because the kind of paper and the covers they were given to print was unusual for them. The books were arty and they liked the challenge. Some of the colours, for instance the blue on *Nine Enclosures*, began to chip, there were sudden white patches. We discovered this a bit late. So future covers used a background which wasn't dense, used lighter colours. Arun wasn't happy with the way his cover for Arvind turned out. He wanted a second go at it and I said, 'We just don't have the money.' I had to think about finances. I had to deal with the bills. My father generously gave me 5,000 rupees to start the thing and the rest we tried to get through pre-order. Here again, firstly, I wasn't responsible for the decision to publish 750 copies of each book, which

Books published by Clearing House in 1976

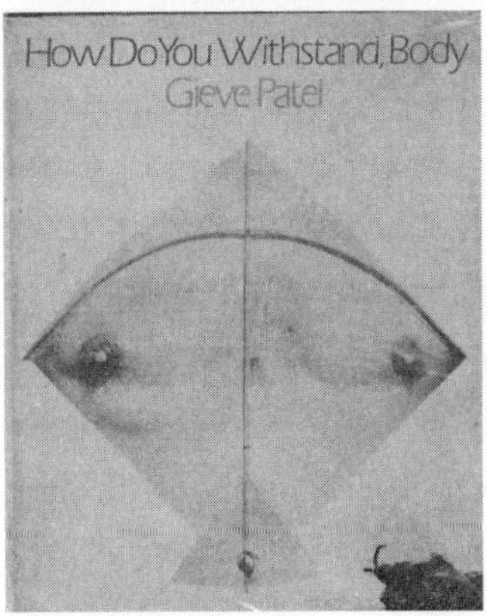

is unusual, it's normally 1,000 or 2,000. Printers would say 750 is not cost effective. Right at the start, to avoid bad blood, we decided not to make decisions based on majority but consensus. Everyone must agree. Ullu that I am, my foolishness lay in the pricing of the first four books. The market price was 12.50 rupees for each book. But my pre-order offer was around 6 rupees for each book. We thought we'd sell abroad as well. For the UK, £1.50 or the equivalent, and for the US, $3. That may have been reasonable but my folly was offering all four books on pre-order for around 6 rupees each. We got about 350 pre-orders for all four books. Not bad, almost 50 per cent. We didn't charge postage. They went to small places in India. Veronik was a great help, addressing packages, visiting post offices. The artists Arun employed did their work gratis. People offered to help free because they thought this was an unusual venture. It was bold, we didn't go through bookshops. It was a nightmare dealing with bookshops, then and now. Strand didn't care to display poetry up front. It was only when Rafiq Baghdadi started to manage Jaico Book Store that he made sure the

Clearing House books were displayed prominently. Mail order wasn't new for people dealing with books in Bombay. But for a start-up venture I think it was bold because it was a way of getting books to places where books wouldn't normally reach: small-town India.

You speak of community, but the poets who were on our mailing lists, university libraries, and the English departments at universities, were largely absent from our list of buyers. We are not as generous with one another as we are led to believe. It's okay to believe in the community of poets but that little bit of effort to buy one another's books doesn't seem to happen. The main bulk of subscribers were in the fields of advertising and theatre, friends of friends. Just to round this off, the pre-orders for subsequent books dropped dramatically. It was a novelty—good-looking books—and then that was it. The same people we'd sent the fliers to just didn't respond to the next two books, Dilip Chitre's *Travelling in a Cage* and Jayanta Mahapatra's *The False Start*. Saleem Peeradina offered the manuscript of his first book, *First Offence*, to us. I knew Saleem quite well and so did Gieve. I don't think that influenced our feeling that we should publish him. But Arvind flatly said no. Arun as usual didn't say anything. His business was to make the book look good, get the best paper and design. He didn't much care about content. Saleem was upset. But since Arun's Clearing House format had caught on, Saleem brought out *First Offence* through another small press using that squarish format. 1976 was a pivotal year. Strangely, the Emergency didn't impact what we were doing at Clearing House, nor was it a cause for setting it up. Oxford University Press (OUP) started its poetry series in 1976—R. Parthasarathy was published, Shiv Kumar was published. A lot of books were published until that absurd decision of the parent OUP not to publish any more poetry. Clearing House wasn't a trigger for OUP, I think it was a coincidence. Jayanta's and Dilip's books came out in 1980. We then published Arvind's *Distance in Statute Miles* in 1982. Arun's cover made Arvind's profile look like part of an archipelago or island. The last book Clearing House published was H.O. Nazareth's *Lobo* (1984). I'd met him in Bombay in 1967. Then he moved to London and got various jobs. I think he'd already started something to do with TV called *Penumbra*. He got funding from what was called the Greater London Council at that time. This was at a time when London bookshops were finally beginning to think about diversity. Because of *Lobo,* some of our Clearing House books got into one or two London bookshops. Because of *Missing Person*, I got invited to the International Writing Program (in Iowa). I took whatever Clearing House books I could to flog them there. The small press movement had started and Clearing House books were announced in small-press newsletters. We got some publicity.

TE: When I asked the question about community, I was expecting you to say there wasn't much of it: *Missing Person* (1976) is a chronicle, among other things, of isolation, alienation.

AJ: Yes, but not due to the author feeling that he lacked a community of poets. The missing person is a paradox. Does he want to be found, or does he want to be invisible, or on the margin? I think the tearing apart of the protagonist in the poem isn't entirely autobiographical. His tearing apart, like

Orpheus being torn apart, has to do with politicization and class. What led to *Missing Person* was that I'd encountered radical left-wing ideas and Marxist theories in Bombay in the early seventies, in study groups, the Progressive Youth Movement, for example. My disillusionment with Marxism had to do with this business of declassing yourself. It's so easily said, but it doesn't happen unless you give up everything that has made you what you are, give up your urban life and love of the arts for something committed and austere. (Renunciation, like Jian's, once again?) So, the protagonist's dilemma is really that. There are mentions of drought in the first part of *Missing Person* because the drought in Maharashtra in 1972–73 affected me greatly, seeing these farmers who'd landed up in the city, not even knowing how to beg, not even putting their hands out, just standing there hoping for help. Along with members of the Progressive Youth Movement, I'd visited a drought-stricken area in Maharashtra. All this made me realize that I had to do what I could from where I was, I couldn't be in the thick of it. But the responses to *Missing Person* among the poets in Bombay were not very favourable. I think the idea that poetry should have nothing to do with politics, an idea which still has a lot of force among poets, had something to do with it. This was not the kind of verse they could warm to. People have called the poem jagged. It's jagged in its lines, it appears so visually, but I must point out there are half-rhymes and assonance, a lyricism which people miss but which could be brought out when the poem is read in public.

TE: Some of the reviews of *Missing Person* were missing themselves, in that they missed the point. How do you respond to negative or uncomprehending criticism?
AJ: I don't think there were very many reviews, apart from Nissim's. Bruce King's was somewhat bland, it wasn't critical. But then I try not to judge my critics or reviewers publicly. I only respond publicly if there's an error of fact, when there's a fair degree of error.

TE: How about privately?
AJ: Well, I guess on first reading I don't get a good feeling, but quite soon I shrug and say, that's the way it is. I'd been

very critical in my own reviews of books that came my way, Indian writing in English, for example. Naturally the writers concerned defended themselves. My theatre reviews were also harsh.

TE: Do you regret that?

AJ: When I wrote them at thirty-something my tone was harsh. If I wrote them now, perhaps not. The thing is, being exposed to ideas and the arts abroad, let's say, in Britain or America, and then returning to India, experiencing those arts in another context, what I learned and I'm suggesting what Nissim and Dom learned as well, naturally has shaped our approach to the arts as they're practised in Bombay. Would I have responded the way I did to a theatre production, an amateur theatre production, if I'd never left India? There was a group called SCADAMS—Santa Cruz Amateur Dramatics and Musical Society. The show may have been called *The Black and White Minstrel Show*, a musical, where you have Indian actors in blackface. (I don't know if I'm being uncomprehendingly snooty, but I still cringe when

Christmas is celebrated here—waiters in Santa caps. Maybe I'm not empathizing enough but it's too much for me.) Anyway, I wrote a review criticizing this kind of mimicry in *The Times Weekly*, I called it 'Black Spots on Brown Sahibs'. It got furious letters. Who is the brown sahib here, them or me? Fair enough, but that clearly hit a nerve. All this is simply as a rejoinder to your question, 'How did I take nasty criticism of my work?' Criticism is a must. I don't regret it. What we believe to be modern and up to date and cutting edge is often nothing more than mimicry. In Naipaul's terms, we continue to be mimic men in reactionary and unprogressive ways.

TE: Do you consider yourself a Leftist?
AJ: *(Pause.)* What?

TE: Do you consider yourself a Leftist?
AJ: Yes, I think I still do, but I do find, or I have found as time has gone by, that some aspects of Marxist theory are questionable, at least I question them and I'm sure others do as well. Similarly, I find certain things disturbingly

wrong about Freud's theories. But I do still consider myself a Leftist. I know 'Left-Liberal' stinks to high heaven these days, everyone thinks it the wimpiest of options. I don't think I'm a Left-Liberal. I may not like people very much but that's common among Humanists, many people who consider themselves Humanists don't like human company. The Humanist idea appeals to me, I'm drawn to it. But I don't know how to define myself, it's impossible. A Humanist with Leftist leanings? Weak, I know, but it's better than being dogmatic about my identity. I don't like to think of identity as being too fluid, as many people do these days. A person I regard as a Humanist, without necessarily finding the pagan Greek writers fundamental to their Humanism, is E.M. Forster. I do believe in what he said: Kindness, kindness and still more kindness. Veronik and I were at Leela's place after Dom had absconded. She wanted to meet us. I said something I felt about myself, that we believe in kindness, kindness and still more kindness, but what we perform is cruelty, cruelty and still more cruelty. Veronik nodded vigorously and Leela said, 'Well said.' It set me thinking about the limits of kindness. I think there's a link between kindness and cruelty. You can be kind to some and cruel to others, including yourself. I don't know where that puts me on the ideological spectrum, in the loony bin probably.

I'm sorry about the pause. When you asked your question, I thought you said, 'Do you consider yourself a lesbian?'

TE: I didn't want to bring it up, but *do* you consider yourself a lesbian?
AJ: No.

TE: Let's get back to identity, in particular to sexual identity.
AJ: My physical experience of sex took place long after puberty. I reached puberty earlier than most boys. I quickly shot up in height which enabled me to win at school races. I could now come first, whereas a few years earlier, I would come last. It enabled me to keep my boxing rivals at bay. All I had to do was stretch out my left hand and they couldn't reach me. The fact that I was ignorant of what sex was, meant

that I had my first sexual experience when I was nineteen, in London. In my years in kindergarten, I was attracted to some girls. I even remember an incident, walking side by side down a little corridor that led to the exit. Outside the gate, various domestic helps were waiting to take their charges home and they were laughing a great deal because I'd grabbed her and kissed her on the cheek. She had black hair going down the side of her head in ringlets. I wasn't slapped, so I suppose it must have been okay with her. The same year, we learned the alphabet through illustrated charts. I used to look at a particular picture—I can't recall what it was—and get a strange feeling in my groin. I was three or four. Later, when I was growing up, before my teens, I developed a crush on my best friend at that time, and later I had a crush on each of his sisters. What I'm getting at is, these were stirrings of bisexuality. I wasn't very good at analyzing these things. There are a few people who might know of my desire for someone of my own sex but I could not recognize myself in whatever Hoshang Merchant has written about my sexuality in the chapter in his book *Gay Icons of India* (2019). I have no problem in calling myself bisexual, but to see myself as a gay icon? I've not hidden the gay element in a few of my poems, not even in *Land's End*. It's there. It's veiled, but later it becomes more explicit. A few of my poems speak of gay emotion or obsession. Hoshang was so determined to prove I was gay, he called my marriage a charade, and that was something I couldn't allow to pass. But this is what happens when you take things for granted. Some gay activists are anxious to prove that the person they have an eye on, though married, is basically gay, and that all heterosexual men are imposters. If you're being dogmatic about it, if it becomes a principle, it doesn't explain the feelings of love and jealousy when a bisexual is in a heterosexual marriage or partnership. For the dogmatists, it's always one way or the other: they believe bisexuality is a cop-out. People also don't realize what happens as you age, the kind of strange desires you have to deal with. The way people speak of fluid identities these days! You think this way when you're young, but you can't go on being fluid. Like heavily promiscuous people can't go on being promiscuous. Maybe I'm just being conservative when I talk about these matters, particularly gay ideologies. But I can't sit in judgement. While sexual orientation isn't necessarily fluid, it's certainly not one or the other. It's not polarized, either heterosexual or homosexual. People have to consider the evidence and not see things in this awful black-and-white way. If you have an axe to grind that is what happens, what else can I say?

TE: What were some of the jobs you held that you'd rather not remember?

AJ: I don't mind talking about those jobs. I remember there was an employment agency called the Brook Street Bureau. I think they sent out people on a daily wage basis, as cleaners. I did a bit of that, cleaning carpets, polishing this surface or that in strangers' homes. I was a supply teacher for a while, in schools with working-class and middle-class students, and students with learning difficulties. Then, I had a job in the sorting department as a sorter of mail at the Shell-Mex building in London, on the South Embankment. A writer there did ask, 'You went to Oxford, what are you

Selfie, circa 1965

Photograph by Adil Jussawalla

doing here?' (One good thing about that place, it had a nice self-serve canteen.) I also was part of a service that filed clippings in different categories. For students who were hard up during the vacations, there were always ways of earning extra money. One of them was by sorting and delivering mail during the holiday season. I did some of that. I know that friends who were at Cambridge worked at post offices during the Christmas season. Darryl D'Monte used to tell me how some employees used to throw their heavy loads into the Thames. Both of us were horrified. My first job must have been during the winter of my first year in London, when I was living in digs and always short of money. In the winter, over the Christmas season, I was employed by a company that used to make and pack Christmas gifts. Their speciality was a kit for making a doll's house. The factory and packing departments were in a building in the working-class part of London. There were young women at their sewing machines on a mezzanine floor, cutting out fabric, making clothes above us packers, and their work was sent down to us, mostly foreigners and people of colour. Flirtatious looks were exchanged by the men in the packing department and the women above us, but at least in my case, nothing ever went very far. There was a tall Black man who used to work alongside me. I suppose he realized from the way I spoke English that I was better educated than him, and when it came to pay time, he thought that he'd been cheated. We must have been paid according to piece work, how many kits you packed in a day, and he asked me to put in a word with the bosses, which I did, duty-bound Indian as I was. I did feel that they hadn't been fair. They heard me out, but I don't think they changed their minds. Race in one way or the other, issues of race, were there from the start, what we used to call colour problems or colour prejudice in Bombay. We never called it race here. All this is reflected in some of the poems in *Trying to Say Goodbye* (2011).

TE: How was your relationship with Dom Moraes? You knew about him when he was at St. Mary's.

AJ: From a student at St. Mary's, Jal Aria, who later studied to be an architect in Sweden. I remember him saying that there was a fantastic student in his class who wrote beautifully and was being published in the school magazine. He mentioned the name, Dom. I thought that Dom and his father were living almost directly opposite where we stayed on Warden Road, in Mafatlal Park, a colony of houses. But I was wrong. Apparently, the photographer Marilyn Silverstone lived there, and perhaps I'd heard from my father that Frank Moraes used to visit. Then, of course, the Indian papers reported that Dom had won the Hawthornden Prize. I was in London at the time. My parents, bless them, sent me a clipping. In England, I'd see a poem of Dom's here and there, in *The Listener*, the BBC magazine, for example. Then, in the few months between my leaving Felsham House and going up to Oxford, I stayed in a bedsit in Chelsea. I walked into a pub, I think the Chelsea Arms. In British pubs, there was the public section and the salon. Well, in this particular pub, you could see across the bartenders, into either section. The salon-wallahs could look into the public and the other way around. I was nursing a pint and I saw, unmistakably, Dom in the salon section. He had a long overcoat on and

I decided I'd risk introducing myself. I went across and asked, 'Are you Dom Moraes?' He looked at me and said, 'Yes, who are you?' I said, 'I write poems,' and that I'd read his poems, and we got chatting. He was friendly, and as he got into his drinks, he forgot he had an appointment. As we were walking down the Chelsea embankment, who should we see but a man striding towards us with furious steps. In a temper, he asked Dom, 'Where were you?' He was George Barker. He'd been waiting at another pub down the road and Dom had just let the time go by. Dom introduced me, as he does, as a poet, fortunately not as a great poet, which he tends to do with strangers. That was my first encounter with Dom. I hadn't got a book out yet. When I went up to Oxford, I found the younger poets had little time for the kind of poetry Dom wrote. They were into the Movement Poets, the deliberately unromantic stance those poets took, quite opposed to Dom's. We must have met again for me to give him a copy of *Land's End* after I went back to Oxford. I remember meeting him and Judith. I thought she was a lovely person. I was charmed by her. Dom was making films for British television. One of them was called *Mighty and Mystical*, about India. Judith must have got involved in one or the other because she wrote to me and said that an American company, Allan King Productions, had a great deal of footage of a train journey from Bombay to Calcutta. He'd called the proposed film *Train to Calcutta*, and she said, quite openly, that they'd asked V.S. Naipaul if he'd write the narrative for it and he'd said no, and so she was asking me. I said okay. It was interestingly shot and I thought what I'd do is pretend I was one of the passengers on the train. There's an encounter with Harindranath Chattopadhyay, one of its passengers. I'm the insider-outsider. So, I sent my narrative to Allan King and his team, but to my horror they said, 'You narrate it.' I went to the studio and I quite liked the way it turned out. It was Judith's doing—she was a kind person. I'm pretty sure the woman in *John Nobody* (Dom Moraes's third book of poems, 1965), the woman brooding over her drink 'like some herbivore', was Judy.

Dom, when he was in Delhi, was more out of it than when he was in Bombay. He was living off a reputation, which got him into the good and bad books of Indira Gandhi. He was asked to speak about Indian poets at the India International Centre in Delhi. I'd sent him the manuscript of *Missing Person*. He said at the lecture that he thought the poem didn't come up to the mark of those in *Land's End*. He said they seemed more like signals of distress than poems. In Bombay, Dom and I didn't meet very often. I'm fond of Dom but I never knew quite where I stood in my friendship with him. Veronik established a French connection with Leela. They were close and talked a lot, in French. I don't know what they talked about. That complicated matters: things weren't going too well between Leela and Dom and I certainly didn't want to get caught in the crossfire. Dom got me a job as book reviews editor for *The Sunday Standard*. He was its editor. That's where you and I met.

TE: You gave me books to review.

AJ: I think he wanted someone more knowledgeable about books and writing than the staff he had for the *Standard*. I introduced new things and Dom said Goenka said, 'What is this man doing, introducing columns by new writers?' I remember publishing a review by Arvind Krishna Mehrotra on the *Oxford India Dictionary* that was so long I had to carry it in two parts. I never knew what Dom was thinking. I remember Dom, Leela and I were in a taxi around the Fort area and him saying that I should write his biography. He often felt misunderstood. He probably thought I'd understand him better. Leela was outraged. She said, 'Dom, how can you say that?' At that time Leela was editing *Keynote*. Manohar Shetty was the literary editor and he said, 'Do a column for us.' Which may be why the three of us were in a cab, going somewhere from the *Keynote* office. Leela's parents were alive and they came from a different world. Dom must have found it hard to be in that apartment. Then things just disintegrated between Leela and Dom, and he left for Sarayu. I think there's some hostility on both sides in my relationship with Dom. It's just that I couldn't quite place him. What was going on in his mind? Who was I to him? Was I a fellow poet or something else? He was never openly hostile, not to my face, but he was suspicious of me.

As writers, we can't always be on the same page. Whenever I've had to review Dom, my review has been favourable. Sometimes I go back to his work and things I liked a lot I feel less sure of now. But I still feel that the final things he wrote, the sonnets, are very, very fine.

TE: You and Nissim Ezekiel were friends for decades.
AJ: I'll begin by saying that our friendship remained intact till the very end despite it being strained from time to time. Our different politics got in the way. I told you about my Leftist leanings and Nissim had long abandoned those. He was now in the liberal camp, for free enterprise, staunchly anti-communist. But that isn't what strained the friendship. It was also the conflicts I was trying to express in the poem 'Missing Person'. He didn't quite understand, or wasn't sympathetic to, what had gotten into me because his review of the book overall was critical and self-confessedly uncomprehending. Clearly, my poetics had changed from the more formal verses of *Land's End*. I think *Missing Person* wasn't measured enough for him, though in exasperation,

at the end of the review, he put in a good word and said it was a breakthrough. But a breakthrough to what, he didn't explain.

People tend to forget that Nissim went to Birkbeck College and he spent three years in London. My theory is that, as with Dom, Nissim's poetry began to be written in the crucible of London's Modernist present. It was the mid-forties: Nissim would have written a very different kind of poetry if he'd never left India. This isn't talked of much. Those three years are more or less a blank, except for a few poems. He was published by the Fortune Press, as were other Indian poets; a vanity press. You had to pay to be published. In Bombay, there was an incident at Nissim's ground floor flat, which Parthasarathy has written about, after the reading of the Beats—Orlovsky, Ginsberg and Snyder—in April 1962. The reading took place at the terrace theatre which Ebrahim Alkazi had constructed above his own flat. It was there, in Bombay, that Ginsberg read his poem 'Kaddish' publicly for the first time. Ginsberg and Orlovsky were interested in what we had written in English, we being the few writers at that reading, Nissim, Parthasarathy, Lancelot Ribeiro and myself. We trooped down Warden Road towards Nissim's flat and the first thing Ginsberg said when he entered and saw a tall shelf full of books in Nissim's small living room, was, 'Books, so many books, what are you going to do with so many books?' Nissim wasn't ever one to react, he kept a straight face. Before we got down to reading our poems, Orlovsky wanted to take a leak. He rushed out on to a sloping lawn and Daisy Ezekiel got most agitated. She sent someone out to bring him back and say there was a toilet in the flat. We tend to accept such behaviour from poets and other weirdos from abroad. If they were Americans in Brooks Brothers suits, we'd find them insulting. It would be like telling us, 'You Indians don't have toilets, you shit in the open.' The Beats were proselytizers. They wanted everyone to write their kind of poetry. They made that clear after the reading. Ginsberg said this kind of formal poetry wasn't suitable for India. You must write differently. He wasn't vehement about it. Orlovsky leaned towards me and said, 'If we were gangster poets we would shoot you.' Ginsberg denied this later. He said Orlovsky never said such a thing. But he wasn't within earshot. This was said to me privately by Orlovsky.

Nissim was disappointed in some things I said in a piece I'd written for *The Journal of Commonwealth Literature*. I'd called it 'The New Poetry' and I looked at Nissim, Lawrence Bantleman, Kamala Das and I don't remember who else. I wasn't being mischievous, I really felt what I said, that I was disappointed in the way poets I admired at a certain time were writing now. Nissim has this oft-quoted poem 'Poet, Lover, Birdwatcher' and I'm surprised that women who cannot be uninfluenced by feminism continue to swoon over it. What I found jarring was simply one word, but that's what can make all the difference in a poem, can't it? There were three lines, 'And there the women slowly turn around / Not only flesh and blood but myths of light / With darkness at the core.' Somewhere, early in that piece, I go to town on Aurobindo's 'Savitri', saying it was 'a vast onion of a poem, its layers gradually fall away to reveal nothing'. So when I read 'myths of light', I felt Nissim was slipping into the Aurobindian mode. He didn't rebuke me, but said, sternly, 'Just because I use one word doesn't make me Aurobindian.' Our friendship remained intact. He had to contend with the fact, as all of us do, that we have minds of our own and we have to accept that if the friendship is to continue.

Another point of stress was later when I was back in Bombay with Veronik and Katia at our flat in Palm Springs. The Ezekiel family had moved into a building called Kala Niketan, which was not at all far from the building where my parents stayed. There was a narrow lane connecting the two spaces. I'd see Daisy walking down and we'd wave at each other. Then Daisy stopped going out in public. I think the story was she was ashamed of her leucoderma. But she did phone my mother often and sometimes even drop in to complain about Nissim. There are days when we can't deal well with the complaints of others. So, my mother said, 'If you're so fed up, why don't you divorce him?' That was the worst thing she could have said. From Daisy's way of thinking, Jews don't divorce. She felt my mother had said something that her religion forbade. Daisy said, 'From now on you're not my friend.' This kind of tension, verbally expressed, must have affected Nissim in some way, because he had become a family friend. He was an in-patient at my father's clinic for a while. I don't know what he must have been there for, just general rejuvenation or something.

Nissim had a base in the old rental flat at Bellasis Road in Byculla. That is where he normally made his way after visiting Daisy, which he was expected to do every day, to bring her provisions mostly. He wasn't permitted to stay in the flat at Kala Niketan, so he'd make his way to Bellasis Road. And from there, next morning, he'd come to South Bombay by train, leaving home early to avoid the rush, waiting on a bench at Churchgate station, marking time before the rooms he had at the PEN Centre at Theosophy Hall opened. People who saw him sitting at the station would make all kinds of moralistic remarks in the press. 'Is this the way a poet should be treated?' 'What's his family doing?' Whatever may be said against R. Raj Rao's biography, for me it's a valuable book. It has a lot of details of that time. I used to visit Nissim often at his PEN office and he was always welcoming. When Veronik and I got married, we had a reception at our flat with an improvised meal and drinks. It was pouring that evening, Cuffe Parade would get totally flooded, become what I used to call the River Cuffe. How would our guests get home? They couldn't. A handful stayed over and they managed with extra mattresses, pillows, blankets. Raj Rao's book says Nissim was among them, but by then I'd forgotten. Eventually, we left the guests to their own devices—I said devices, Jeet, not vices—and retired. After all, it was our wedding night.

There was another dramatic overnight stay of Nissim's at the flat at Palm Springs. This was in early 1993, January, post-Babri Masjid, which led to the riots in Bombay. Also, those massive explosions all over the city. My father had had a bad fall and broken his thigh bone. He was convalescing at his home at Warden Road after being hospitalized. I used to visit him through the devastation of the city. The building my parents live in, is approached through a slope going upward from the main road. At one point it's quite steep. I was going down that slope to take a taxi to return to my flat in Cuffe Parade. As I approached the main road, I saw Nissim walking past in the direction of Byculla. He had visited Daisy and was going back. I asked him, 'How on earth are you going to go back, what transport will you get?' He said, 'I'll find something.' I said, 'Nothing doing, come with me, Veronik is in France and you can stay in her room.' He came over and stayed. During the night, I heard much shouting and I went to the balcony to look out. There were people running down the street chasing someone. To my horror, I saw a body being dragged out of our building through its gate, leaving streaks of blood on the paving stones, like tyre marks. It seems that a group up the road had made fun of an aarti going on in the fishermen's colony and that led to the people involved in the aarti to give chase to those who mocked it, and at least one person had been killed. I was employed as the book reviews editor for *The Sunday Review* of *The Times of India*. I remember ringing the *Times* and saying I want to report this happened, maybe someone should investigate. No one did. It would have been wrong of me to have woken Nissim, so he slept through it all. In the morning, he insisted on going to Theosophy Hall unaccompanied. The riots returned after the Pakistan-inspired attacks on Bombay. Inevitably for me, *Gulestan* (2017) had to be written. The poem questions what's sacred, not just inside me, but outside. Are there any sacred places? It's like they're all being overrun by hatred and dreadful ideologies.

Even if you go through his *Collected Poems*, however slowly, even when taking up a section of the book, I find reading Nissim and rereading Nissim rewarding. It's poetry of a very high quality. I don't myself subscribe to denouncing Nissim's work, though it's fashionable to do so in some quarters.

TE: You and Eunice de Souza also had a long friendship.
AJ: I really have no recollection of when we first met. She wasn't writing poetry and she and Veronik got on well. This is the early seventies. A friendship developed. She had sharp and intelligent things to say about writing and

people. Then, she started writing poems and would show them to me. If I were to say something thoughtless about Veronik, like calling her Whitey, she would naturally take Veronik's side and I'd be ticked off. I was never really sure what would offend Eunice and offend her badly. I wasn't the subject of any of her sharp rebuking letters. If she went away hurt, she tended to send letters to those who had hurt her. As time went by, Veronik too received one or two. With Clearing House, we were committed to publishing Eunice but we didn't have funds, so we had to wait. Eunice got impatient and took her manuscript to Newground, which was being run by her student and friend Melanie Silgardo, with Santan Rodrigues and Raul D'Gama Rose.

I used to teach English language courses in Bombay, lessons which I myself had devised, based on the direct method I taught at the International House in London. I don't know if I suggested it or Eunice did, but I said there are what people used to condescendingly call 'vernacs' at Xavier's, where Eunice was teaching, and

Elphinstone, so why not take the course to them after their lectures? Eunice put in a word with the head of the English department of St. Xavier's, and I did teach there for a while, at least a year, and then there was a vacancy in the English department and Eunice suggested I go for it and become a teacher of English literature. That's how I began teaching English literature at St. Xavier's. She was always very helpful, but she didn't like the way literature was taught and the ideas of some of the teachers in the department. Eunice was independent, she made her mind known. Let's say there wasn't a warm community of Eng Lit teachers in the staffroom.

The early seventies was a time of turmoil. People weren't happy with the Congress party's policies. There were protests and morchas. Teachers, too, protested for better pay. I wasn't confirmed at Xavier's. You had to teach for two years before they decided to confirm you. But it was a great time. I think I was popular as a teacher because of the direct teaching method. But the English language teaching classes, the students attending them, dwindled.

They wanted coaching in their major subject, as in what answers to give in Physics, Chemistry, so they attended those coaching classes rather than mine. After a while, they decided not to carry on with the English language classes. But I held informal classes of another kind near the canteen. I tried to introduce poets and writers who were not on the syllabus—Arvind's work, the Beats, etc. They were well attended. After my two years at Xavier's, the business of my being confirmed came up. I wasn't called to a meeting or anything, but I was told that I hadn't been confirmed. Xavier's new principal was suspicious of my association with Leftists. The Progressive Youth Movement I was associated with put up an exhibition in one of Xavier's quads, pointing out the failures in the government's agricultural policies. Eunice was upset when she heard I wasn't confirmed. Nissim was head of the department at the university. They both wrote letters supporting me and I got confirmed. But then, it was my doing that I left the college a year later, a repetition of what happened with architecture. I left architecture to write a play, and here I left college to write a novel, not aware, then, that it would be one more failure.

I soon realized the novel wouldn't work. I'd got the form wrong. The story of a foreign-returned photographer, Dali Kabraji, who went by the pseudonym Dolly Cobra and had been commissioned to do a book on the monsoon. But in 1972–73, the monsoon had failed and there was immense suffering in Maharashtra. This led to the politicization of Dolly Cobra. He wanted to document the drought.

After I left Xavier's, Eunice and I met very often. She became a columnist at *The Economic Times*. We had common friends. As with all friendships there were ups and downs, but nothing that couldn't be sorted out. She didn't like me using the word 'transcend'. I had tried to say that at times in our writing we had to go beyond the personal and I may have used the word 'transcend'. But she didn't send me a letter, she got her response down in a poem, as she had when she'd addressed a poem to Nissim. You'll find the poem in *Fix*. It begins, 'Transcend something ...' In time, tiffs and misunderstandings were forgiven, the friendship lasted right till the end. Unfortunately, she passed away just two days before Veronik and I were to leave for France. There was no way we could have cancelled our flight. Katia got into Xavier's and she chose Eng Lit as her subject. I'll mention that she found Nisha da Cunha's personality and way of teaching more sympathetic that Eunice's. Nisha was head of department. She and Eunice were sometimes barely on speaking terms. I really wish Eunice's prose, her columns, the things she wrote for *The Times of India* and *The Economic Times*, I wish a selection were published because it gives you a clear idea of what was happening culturally over three decades.

She had an uncanny instinct about what I would like as gifts and which books I would like to review. I don't know how Eunice knew but when she was book reviews editor for *Indian Post*, whatever books she sent me I could not refuse to review. Their contents fascinated me. Also, in her gifts, she chose something she knew I would take to. She had this instinct.

TE: There was a long period when you didn't publish a book of poetry, thirty-five years, and then this incredible flowering over the past decade.

AJ: I *was* writing poems and they were published here and there. It's what happens to some people. The business of being a householder, of earning a living, writing columns, not just for one newspaper, but quite a few. Veronik found my need to be isolated difficult, she couldn't take it. One of her French friends was working for Air France and she had a two-bedroom flat with a large living room in Churchgate, just above the Chinese restaurant there. Veronik said it would also bring her friend some money if I rented out the hall as my workspace for the day. I did use that hall for a couple of years and worked on the novel. Friends would drop in and see me. It led to drinking, and writing was often forgotten for conviviality.

TE: I remember. You frequented Gokul, the bar behind the Taj, where alcohol was sold by the quarter bottle and poets and millworkers drank together. When did you stop drinking?

AJ: I gave up smoking before I gave up drinking, long before, because I'd become almost a chain-smoker, and Veronik, too, was a smoker. Strangely, it was a meeting with Vijay Nambisan that did it. We had a late evening and, in the morning, just the sight of all those ashtrays and stubbed cigarettes seemed so awful that I decided to stop smoking. I followed the advice of *Quit*, a little booklet, the cold turkey method, just stop and have faith that you converted from being a smoker to being a non-smoker. It's almost like a religious conversion or perhaps it *is* a religious conversion. If you have faith in your life now, you don't slip back. That served me very well. And though, when I felt stressed, there was a feeling to reach out for a pack, I didn't succumb. Ten years later, I decided to follow the same thing when it came to my drinking. Just stop cold. Again, it was a matter of faith. I decided to test this the next day. I used to take away food from Gokul and its sister bar in Fountain, Amrapali. I found no temptation to order a drink at Amrapali when I deliberately went there and I felt very good about that.

TE: Roughly when was this?

AJ: March 1999. I wasn't paying attention to the drafts of poems. I let them lie and didn't do anything with them. But it wasn't the drinking, it was something else to do with my character, probably something to do with my editorial and organizational side. What happened was that the freedom and the rush of energy I got after giving up drinking heavily, led me to organize things, for example the Loquations programme at the National Centre for the Performing Arts' Chauraha. Toni Patel, Gieve's wife, passed, and I found myself organizing 'Toni's Day', a mix of play readings and art, at a newish art gallery. All this should indicate that my heart was still not in completing the poems I'd written, or even in writing prose. But by that time, I did have columns to write, one for *Keynote*, another for Yogi Aggarwal's Associated News Features. I was still far away from *Trying to Say Goodbye* which was published in 2011. There was an event organized by Almost Island. I read the few poems I thought were complete and

Sharmistha Mohanty said, 'If you have a manuscript, we'd like to publish you.' That did it.

TE: And now here we are, publishing something you wrote at age eighteen or thereabouts, formatted differently from the way you originally wrote it.
AJ: Well, you have my permission for that.

TE: Are you sure?
AJ: Sure I'm sure.

Some parts of this conversation originally appeared in South Parade, *Vol. 1, 2024.*

Photographs courtesy Adil Jussawalla and The Guild.

Soliloquies

My Father?
This bastard father intrudes as always
Nothing's been gained but
Pain and fear and illusion,
Dissolution, darkness, despair—
These things affect me still—growing
Around me stronger than before—
And strangling.

†

When after walking my own shadow for
Years, I broke from it and fell
Into a visioned universe of light,
Blinded, shadowless and true, only to
Fall back to earth and live
Newly conscious; newly born
Out of darkness into light and
Deepest darkness again. For that is
What knowledge is: the shadow

Following the enlightenment, the
Responsibility following the response, the
Obedience following the command.

But where does my obedience lie?
Is the command given in these
Voices of the past, all screaming
To be heard, or in an
Unknown silence, revealing what
Remains unknown for me and earth,
And which, when known, could give peace
Here, and being freely given
Give out freely
One pure and simple Truth
To destroy our myriad-mirrored glitter of
Heart-felt lies,
Reflecting to and from ourselves?

I'd obey my voices wherever they'd lead me
But my parents need me too—or so

They make out to appear: They fear
I'm still too young to go to Hell.
To be stripped bare to the evil within me
And unflinchingly face the
Consequences of my discovery. Yet
I will explore the regions of my
Soul, the wastes and the peaks together,
I will know my self so the power to
Rule my self will follow.

Knowledge which began a vast
Cycle at my birth is closing
On itself now. Yet one gap,
One stretch of shadow remains to
Be crossed before the circle's ends
Meet, and fulfil the Plan.

Before I leave my home to start
Another—for that is my way to my
Necessary isolation—that is my

Need for detachment. Still—
God help those downstairs still
Unaware of my intentions to
Leave them; blind to my future except
In the plans they make for it.

Balancing my worth to them every
Day, to see how clearly I can
Divide right and wrong, God and
Un-God in my actions as though
I must be doctor with my gifts and
Judge with my knowledge, for the
Sake of their dream-world,
And a career.

†

But for me
There is one world here, where
Neither division nor marriage, between

One and two, true and false exist
For they are one in truth—
Here is the Light I long for again,
Darkness and the devil can go to Hell.
The kingdom of God is within me.

Father, I ask and keep on asking
But there is no answer.
I ask again, knowing I cannot
Know you, but hoping I cannot hope
To rest until the circle closes
And I hear your
Voice from all things on earth.

What have I to do with earth?
Its soil around my feet hugs me
Like a mother, while its thorns
Slit into my back and spill the
Sap of my surrender.

Now, between my birth and my

Fulfilment, I fall weak, weakened
With fears of tomorrow and cares
That it may not supply my need to
Live, and its evil ravens may
Sip my withering leaves to dip their
Bills in this last upshot of strength.
Hoar frost. Ice thawing in the
Sweep of its flat unfriendly winds.
Wild-bird wings beating out the
Fires of dawn against a smothered sky.

Sun will rise again. Fires will
Warm, but till then why must I be
Left unsatisfied,
Asking and doubting the nature of
What I am, and what around
Me must be?
Tell me
What have I to do with earth
If I cannot hear a truthful

Voice in all it offers me, even
The fruitless thorn?
If the pain it gives
Can't be conquered and the root of
Pain I seek, can't be found?

A pin in space
And countless stars around
And space unsolved—
My point of life is pointless
For earth's solution.
Unborn me now, if all my life is
Spent in peace-less searching for an
Answer which can come only by
Vanishing my question:
Dissolve it like the mountain
                like the airplane lights,
Dissolve it to a silent word.
What have I to do with earth?

†

(Weighed down deep)

O God,
For whom I have to hurt
The ones I love; for whom
    My conscience and my pride
    Must be annulled,
This biting self of mine remove,
    Accept my surrender.
Speak through me your servant
    that my speech may have
    no malice, hate nor anger,
    that egoistic still, my self
    will not interfere.

It is hard for me to live
    for you.

Bitter the sorrow to know illusion.
Bitter the pain to touch a heart
        and know it false,
        when like a moth
        that has undisturbed died
        and for days remains an
        empty skin, its marrow
        crumble at my touch and
All is divided.

Heal this pain of division, Lord,
This parting of ways.
Cannot those I love receive You
Through me, that I must
Leave them to illusion, and know
        Truth myself?

Still only part do I know, and if
Such the hurt of a part, how much
More for the whole?
Was part happiness truer than

This wisdom? Must he that increases
Knowledge increase sorrow, as it
Has been written in Ecclesiastes?

        Prophets,
Now I ask you, if
        this has been your pain
        how were you at peace
        within yourselves?
David, why are your psalms despairing
Over an enemy's reproach?
Siddharth of India, has your
Serene Buddha head no compassion for
Those you forsook?

        But they are dead.
Dust will not stir at groaning
Neither the cities built on it
Answer to show what
Great work they have done: All
That is gone.

So I shall learn too,
No more here where I have
Reached the bottom of my draught—
But in a desert place, foreign
Enough to be a
Wilderness for me.

There is one, calling far from
Home and hope, in a lonely
Land—eating spit, drinking
Tears where no one calls a name
Or asks me where I go,
Where even the earth and all
Natural things shut me out.
There I shall know the deepest griefs of
Man—Tribulation and Temptation both
Coactive.
If then I love you still, God,
Myself shall be absolved, as all
My conscious will shall be, and your
Presence shall stay with me forever.

(He rises,
Moves over
slowly
and pauses
at the
door.)

The time is now
And they must know.
Soften the blow, God.

(A spotlight intrudes into Jian's room, and sweeps over him. He is crosslegged as before, but his clothes have not been cast off, and he is peaceful. He stirs as the light shines on his eyes, then looks at us and speaks.)

Moment upon moment
Hour after hour
Of this have come and gone
Not dreaming   not sleeping   not searching
Neither conscious
Nor unconscious
Nor fanciful
but still
Receiving yet forever still
A knowledge from contemplation

Shall you   when you can

All man   woman and child here
Human enough to understand

the profit and loss of dreams
which haunt you   with Paradise
but refusing it   to you

Listen for a while

There is within
us all   though not a dream
A peace   which despite unprevailing
Laws prevails for you
you
and you that you
may have fulfilment
Not Romance   that is nostalgia
in age   senility   decline
You are only young once
you say   be pampered when
you can   but which man
saying that has not
been taught to say it
by his elder brothers
Re-hashing their youth in philosophies
which today are truthless
except in looking back

For you   becoming Individuals
as you listen   is this
unitive light of Knowledge
and Peace   so that Earth
                                    low pulse
                        as it is in Time
                                    space
                                    cosmos
Throb with your Humanity   shining
Ultimate at last
But not through hell-bent uprisings
            to establish Utopia tomorrow a
            resolution of the will seeking
            revolution for no
            revelation shall be yours
Until your wills are gone

Have you seen a child
            that wanders without it
and stops to stare amazed

at a bird or leaf
A word from us
'It is a bird' or 'A lovely leaf'
and he will turn away
a secret never to be told

For it was him for one eternal
Moment in revelation and to
you
with all your natural history
it is just a silly word
without the great experience

Would you kill your child wilfully
And don't you for however skillfully
you avoid it how can you
deny that it learns more
without a will of its own
Than you who exercise
a willpower over all

even your child   that all
may lead to your given
end of desiring more
even if
It be truth   without letting it
come of its own accord

Not an ounce of your telling
can give a child an inner
faith in his own listening
Keep him from all ignorance
by shutting out his life
with your experience
and he'll scrape the putty
from the cracks and peep
out to find that what is
for him was not for you
And he'll renounce his illusion
even to your last word

So don't be frightened
of what speaks to you for
knowledge of within
and from yourselves
Though the world order you to pander
to one of its
ignorant authorities
Remember you too were a child
living apart
Freely receiving the true nature
of a world made for you
alone
an individual
Until your elders came and
snatched it from you
with laughter kisses a
smack that hurt a call
to obey that you may
Conform to their sub-neutral society
Perverted by degrees past your

Youth and age   what's the vision
before you now
A shadowed stage on which your
Fenced-in figure must play its part
according to another's wishes
or fade away to nothing

Ever be a child awakening
as one that forever opens
its eyes and awakes
Imagine its eternal moment
of revelation
For that is its inheritance of Light
as it is ours from our Father
to us the Son
Immaterial through the Holy Ghost

†

I am   yet
I am not

Not yet lifeless   but
Dying for life

For life again
I will die   and will live
Before the dying
With the dead

This is the world of the dead
And the dying
See   the table empties out its life
Onto the floor   and the floor
into the wall and
The wall is dead already

An aged spirit dies
Heaving up its last breath
On me
It is time for a new one
Again
Again a circle tries to close

(He is
down
by his
bed)

A rebirth's agony is near
Hold me father
It is near
Nearer than my voice is
To my throat
My sight is to my eyes
Hold me Father
It is near
I fear my safety on its
Foreign ground   It has
Empty chasms for my feet

Father stay with me
It is nearer than my cry is
To my calling
It is within and without me
It is closed about me as a
Fist of water
It will choke and spill
It will kill
me Father
Stay

(He PAUSES

looking about

him in fear

Then as though LOST

irretrievably)

I and no other by me
I and by me no other
To brother me in my separation
        On a bat-winged web I am
        Spread and crucified in the
        Sky's dark tomb
                Now the infrangible stretch
                Between death and birth is
                Straddled   and the heaving pull
                        Of both beset me
Night is stronger   night will get me
        With my dying self never
        Reborn into my selflessness

How pale my past adventures seem
When release came easy
        What keeps me still to see that
        I cannot leave before I see it
My eyes turn inwards   strain inwards
And see the desolation   When outwards
In the night   darkness presses on the

Eyelids with a hardened palm
And in the daylight releases to see
Another desolation   sterile, bleak and
Humanless   Whom shall I turn to
Whom shall I call

Spirit who has nurtured me
Spirit unto many spirits and
Life unto many lives
            Who has born and reborn other
            Births into my own
                        Do not abandon me
                        I am as a web crucified
Do not abandon me

Father in Heaven   Spirit of
            All Spirits
            Rebuke me not
I cannot hold these thoughts which ask
Why my rebirth is forbidden me

Turn then not away and
Turn me not to emptiness

Blessed Mother   Spirit of
The earth   of whom I came but part of
Constrain me not
        Nor send the sweat of your
        Humanity to my mouth
Let me be free of bitterness

Winging Sister   Spirit of
The air   changing fast
Yet lasting unchanged
        Waver me not
        Blow softer for my frailty
        Scatter easy into sudden
Confusion

And you Brother   Spirit of
Humanity   waiting out in

Endless waiting for a new home
            Refuse me not
            I am like you to speak
              And listen to
I have waited too

Eternal family
Eternal Spirit woven in
Our bones   be integral with
Me once more
Give back your life to these
Who have lost it   and my own
Loss make me forget with
A greater find
            Eternal family abounding
            Refuse me not my call
                        Turn me not away and
                        Turn me not to emptiness

I have lost all

†

I love you
I love you
                                        You must never leave me
I love you   never leave me
                                        never leave me
                    My God you're possessed
                                        you're possessed

My God you're possessed
My God My God My God
Devil   you're possessed
Devil   you're running away
Devil   from duty
I challenge you   duty
I challenge you   running from duty
                                    Oh Christ it's broken
                                              broken
                                          it's broken
Give me your faith
Give me Give me Give

Give

I have nothing to give
except my voice to   Give
Add to voices   Give
Take it away   Give

Give Give Give
Give Give Give
Give me your faith

My faith is only in
that which gives
Peace Not you deceiving
voices of the ego
haunting like
those that came
in the wood to haunt
Faith scattered you and
not faith in you

(A great clap
sounds, with a
lightning-crack
that splits the
sky apart.
As a hot
glass bowl in
an oven.)

Peace! and let me pray
Be still! I'll give to God
Not you

Now my faith has been given
My self surrendered to You
All evil and good have gone
    with my surrender
I have given to the Unknown
I have given without hope
    of reward or rest
Stillness comes
I feel your silent presence here
The rest will follow

(The lights fade away, Tian is seen sitting still and peaceful in his room. The light on him has an unearthly radiance now. It is the end of his transformation.)

What was missing
Has been found.
The circle has closed.
The rest has followed,
Ended yet unending
And complete.

As words are not in silence,
The highest I can speak is
Not the word but
The Love,
Soundlessly surrendering
To you.
I refused it, and fell, yet
My last cry was for resolving
Love's confusion within me,
And Love has answered me
My cry and given me
This last rebirth here.

When a circle's tract begins
Every point's a turning point,
No point can be without
One gone before or
One following,
Until the last point
Between end and beginning is
Crossed,
End becomes beginning,
Beginning end
And Life and Knowledge are
Fulfilled in the plan.
And as in the beginning
My point of life was born
With Love and lived
For Love so now
It has come back to it.

But at this gap between
Beginning and end I stopped,

Turned away from Love
In defiance
And dropped.

That was my torment:
Good defied, found out the
Evils I denied myself
And they became temptation.
Then the ego's unfed fires
Burned me to depravity
Until I killed them with the
Good I turned away from.
This last remained to be known
To close the circle,
To fulfil the Plan and
Start another:

Hating evil's just another hate.
Loving good is what destroys it.

There is nothing more to
Know in isolation.
The cup is full.
Now it is time to make it
Brimless: and renounce.

I renounce this home,
This family and the shelter
It has given me from the
Chaos outside it.

And for that within it
Only my leaving can solve.

Now when I come to heal you
Do not turn against me.
You are my shelter now, though
Many among you will
Deny me it.
Lies shall try to shout me

Down, or use my words as
A slogan for their truth.
Age shall make youth mock me.
Men shall burn my face with
Fierce lamps and wash my
Brain out in a cruel
Spate of Inquisition.
Till I confess my madness
For having heard God's word.

For as the dark must be lightened
So shall the instruments of
Darkness rise up to destroy me.

Today you listen insensible to
Yesterday's wrongs and
The sorrows beneath your feet,
But tomorrow ...
There's no tomorrow.
Even today shall the desolation

Strike if it must:
Politics, prating of peace intending
War shall be overthrown
By its own intentions and
Religion preaching a peace
Decadent and dissenting
Shall dissolve.

No readjustment will work then.
The lever's balancing point
Shall not be found.
No science will remedy the defect,
For Society's nervous breakdown
Shall not end without a
Nervous annihilation.
A calculation gone wrong,
A mind unbalanced is all
Desolation waits for,
Prepared today to curse
Generations to come.

A long journey lies ahead.
Eternal father, guide me to
The road, and keep me to it.
Send me Temptation, Father
That I may conquer it.
Send me evil
That I may crush it.

And grant me the strength
To heal all who have suffered it.

(Is all Life asleep?
Drowned by relief
and this strange hum
that grows from all
around, the three
downstairs are asleep.
Is all Life asleep to
the action that must
follow? The light
around the room has
grown unearthly.
Is it all a dream —
a shadow of the
past?)

Sleep on.
You have earned your rest,
This house be blessed,
The shock of leaving will be
Less for you now knowing
That this had to be,
Every action before an
Action sleeps, and every
Action beyond it, lies with
The Unknown.
It is the action itself
Which is the awakening;
So if, through mine, one
Awakens to grief, another to
Happiness, or another to
Punishment,
Accept it as an act
Inevitable in your design.
I am but the instrument.
The will is Eternal, and mine
Has given up to it.

So you cannot be
Misjudged by the Unknown
Sentence on you.
For every will that lies still
Within an unknown Will.
For every action done for an
Unknown good.
Nothing can follow that is evil
For the Will and the Action
Fulfil the Plan, which from
God, though Unknown
Is good.

I leave you now.
May you feel no loss if
You should hear of me
Again and remember
Me: I am still with
You. Love will keep what
Sight and sound will lose.

Forgive me if I had to choose
The Light and not your shadows,
It was my greater love.

As pure as children in your
Separate worlds you lie.
Untouchable, untroubled,
God be with you.

A child's light can never die.

Is all Life asleep? Drowsed by relief and this strange hum that grows from all ground, the three downstairs are asleep. Is all Life asleep to the action that must follow? The light around the room has grown unearthly. Is it all a dream - a shadow of the past?

JIÄN

Sleep on
You have earned your rest
This house be blessed
The shock of leaving will be
Less for you now knowing
That this had to be,
Every action before an
Action sleeps, and every
Action beyond it, lies with
The Unknown.
It is the action itself
Which is the awakening;
So if, through mine, one
Awakes to grief, another to
Happiness, or another to
Punishment
Accept it as an act
Inevitable in your design.
I am but the instrument
The Will is Eternal, and mine
Has given up to it.

So you cannot be
Misjudged by the Unknown
Sentence on you.
For every will that lies still
Within an Unknown Will
For every action done for an
Unknown good
Nothing can follow that is evil
For the Will and the Action
Fulfill the Plan, which from
God, though Unknown
Is good.

I leave you now.
May you feel no loss if
You should hear of me
Again and remember
Me: I am still with
You. Love will keep what
Sight and sound will lose
Forgive me if I had to choose
The Light and not your shadows,
It was my greater love.

As pure as children in your
Separate worlds you lie.
Untouchable, untroubled
God be with you.

A child's light can never die.

Adil Jussawalla was born in 1940 in Bombay. He was educated there and at University College, Oxford. He taught English at the International Language Centre in London, where he met his future wife, Veronik, then returned to Bombay in 1970. Since then, he has been a lecturer at St. Xavier's College, Bombay, and has held editorial positions at *The Indian Express*, *The Times of India*, *Debonair*, *Science Age* and *For You*. He was a columnist for *Keynote*, *Gentleman*, *Sunday Herald* and *The Sunday Observer*, wrote a syndicated fortnightly column for Associated News Features, and edited the influential anthology *New Writing in India* (Penguin, 1974) which predicted an Indian literary future that largely came true in the decades that followed. He was a founding member of the poets' collective, Clearing House, which published eight seminal books of poems between 1976 and 1984, including his own book-length poem, *Missing Person* (1976). He has written for the BBC and Channel 4, was an Honorary Fellow at the University of Iowa's International Writing Program, and has been translated into various Indian and European languages. Adil Jussawalla is the author of seven previous books of poems, *Land's End*, *Missing Person*, *Trying to Say Goodbye* (which was honoured with the Sahitya Akademi Award in 2014), *The Right Kind of Dog*, *Shorelines*, *The Tattooed Teetotaler and Other Wonders* and *It Remains to Be Said;* two poetry chapbooks, *Gulestan* and *Earth*; and four selections of prose, *Maps for a Mortal Moon*, *I Dreamt a Horse Fell from the Sky*, *The Magic Hand of Chance* and *Body of Evidence*.

HarperCollins *Publishers* India

At HarperCollins India, we believe in telling the best stories and finding the widest readership for our books in every format possible. We started publishing in 1992; a great deal has changed since then, but what has remained constant is the passion with which our authors write their books, the love with which readers receive them, and the sheer joy and excitement that we as publishers feel in being a part of the publishing process.

Over the years, we've had the pleasure of publishing some of the finest writing from the subcontinent and around the world, including several award-winning titles and some of the biggest bestsellers in India's publishing history. But nothing has meant more to us than the fact that millions of people have read the books we published, and that somewhere, a book of ours might have made a difference.

As we look to the future, we go back to that one word—a word which has been a driving force for us all these years.

Read.